LUCY H

LITTLE LUCIE

It's up to you to tell the truth!

DEDICATION

To my sons, William and Ritchie. If you want something in life, when you put your mind, heart and soul into it, anything is possible!

The sun was shining and it was a great day to play outdoors. Lucie was extremely excited, as it was the first day of summer and there was no more school, at least not until September. Living on a farm is the perfect place for many new adventures. There are green and brown frogs to catch along with big and small trees to climb. 'Oh!' and how about all those rocks that you get to turn upside down, and discover how many different bugs live under there! Lucie feels the happiest when she is outdoors; she feels a certain connection with everything that involves nature.

Lucie is a nine-year-old little girl, who is excep-
tionally happy and also very creative. She is
thin, with long orange and red hair that she
always wears in two braids. Her braids however
are in a higher than normal place. They are on
the sides of her head. They stick out and look
rather goofy, but this is because Lucie wants to
look different from other people. She believes
that everyone should get to choose the way
they dress, style their hair the way they want
and play with whomever they want. Lucie also
has chubby cheeks that are covered with big
red freckles.

Lucie often wears odd coloured clothing
and always seems to have two odd stockings; one is always shorter than the other is.
Today she is extremely excited because she
can wear her old coveralls that are cut off just
above the knee. They are, without any doubt,

her favourite pair, because they show off her stockings. In a hurry this morning, she put on two different coloured stockings. One stocking was long with red and white stripes the other was short with yellow and green stripes. That doesn't matter to Lucie though because being different is what she liked best.

She lives in the country on a small farm with her mom, Carol. Carol is a single mom, because her husband passed away when Lucie was only two years old. Carol is a rather tall woman with a thin frame. She has short red hair with orange -like streaks; it is always neat and tidy. Although Lucie's mom was raised on a farm, she is a very proper and polite lady.

Lucie is an only child, but she has a big white dog named Ruby. Ruby is a purebred five-year-old Labrador retriever who is slightly on the chubby side. She isn't an ordinary dog; she's Lucie's best friend and confidant. Ruby and Lucie play together all the time. Whether it's in the house or outside, they are rarely ever apart. Lucie tells Ruby all her secrets, like when she hid her broccoli in her dresser until garbage day. She did this so her mom wouldn't know that she wasn't eating it.

One day, her mom gave her brussels sprouts at suppertime and she thought they looked too weird to eat, so she went to hide them. On her way to her bedroom, she was looking at the sprouts and thought to herself, "Maybe I'll take one little bite and see if I like it!" Well, to Lucie's amazement she really did like the taste! They did not make it to Lucie's bedroom or to her hiding place in the dresser with the broccoli. The broccoli would have to stay by itself until garbage day.

The next morning, Lucie decided that since it was nice outside she would go out with Ruby and see if they could find Dot. Dot is also one of Lucie's best friends, a tiny little chipmunk that lives under the back porch of Lucie's old farmhouse. Dot likes to tease Ruby by appearing and then disappearing from under the porch. Lucie has been hand feeding Dot hardshelled peanuts since Dot was a baby. Dot and Lucie have a special bond also, because neither of them has a brother or sister, but at least they have each other.

When Lucie and Ruby finally went outside the back door onto the porch, Dot was sitting there all cute like, almost as if she was anticipating their arrival. Lucie sat down on the first step of the porch. Ruby didn't notice Dot, so she took off running after a squirrel on the fence surrounding the small barn. This was a great moment for Dot, as she would now be able to hop up onto Lucie's lap and enjoy a few peanuts with her best friend.

Once Dot was finished eating her peanuts, she went back underneath the broken porch. As it turned out, it was perfect timing, because at that very moment Ruby was back from her chase with the squirrel. The country has many opportunities for chasing critters. Big or small, Ruby would chase them all.

Lucie and her mother share the small farm that they live on with a few animals. They can be very expensive to keep and provide for. They have four chickens that lay eggs, one rooster and one cow for milk. Lucie has to collect the eggs every morning before school while her mom hand milks the cow.

Lucie enjoyed collecting the eggs, as she would pretend that it was Easter and the hunt would be on. She also had to give the chickens and rooster some grain along with some fresh water. She didn't mind as she enjoyed helping her mom with the chores. Lucie thought, "It can't be work if you enjoy what you're doing!"

Lucie decided it was time to collect the eggs from the chickens that were nestled on some straw in the little old tattered barn. Living on the farm has many opportunities for curious young minds! On her way to the barn, she saw the cow eating grass, and wondered to herself, "How can grass possibly turn into milk inside the cow!" That thought soon left after Ruby started to chase the chickens all around the barn.

Lucie wasn't pleased with Ruby when she saw the mess and broken eggs that were in the straw. Now what would she tell her mom when she went to the house with no eggs for the days gathering! "Oh well!" Lucie thought, "Nothing I can do about it now, what's done is done!" Maybe her mom would handle this situation the same way; at least that is what Lucie was hoping for.

When Lucie was finished cleaning up, she fed the chickens some grain and gave them some fresh water. The cow had her own automatic water bowl and with lots of fresh green grass to eat, there was no need to feed her some grain. Lucie's chores were finished, so she headed back to the house.

She would tell her mom what had taken place between the chickens and Ruby. Lucie was

afraid that her mom might be upset with her for letting Ruby in the barn. She knew the rules; Ruby wasn't allowed near the chickens or in the barn! That day two rules were broken and so were the eggs!

When Lucie walked in the house her mom noticed the egg basket was empty, but she said nothing. This made Lucie wonder if she should say anything to her mom, as the look on her face was one she had seen before. Finally, her mom said to her, "I saw what took place at the barn this morning, with the chickens and Ruby!" Lucie didn't say a word. She could feel her heart pounding in her chest. Then her mom turned around and said, "Young lady, you know you broke two rules this morning and that those eggs are expensive!" For this, you will not get any broccoli as a vegetable this week for supper. I will have to buy eggs with the money I normally use for the broccoli.

On that note, Lucie decided it was best to go to her room and think about the outcome of her breaking the rules. After what seemed like an eternity, she decided to take the broccoli out of her dresser and took it into the kitchen to show her mom. In her heart, she knew that the right thing to do was to tell her mom, and to ask her not to buy brussels sprouts. Lucie told her mom that she likes brussels sprouts but not broccoli, and that she had been hiding the broccoli in her dresser all along!

That day, Lucie's mom knew that her little girl was growing up to into a fine young woman, and an honest one at that. She was very proud of her little girl and wished that her husband could have been there to see how his little girl had handled this situation. Lucie handled it better than most adults would have, with the truth.

Wholesale discounts for book orders are
available through Ingram Distributors.

Tellwell Talent
www.tellwell.ca

ISBN
Paperback: 978-1-988186-49-8

ACKNOWLEDGMENTS

I would like to thank everyone at Tellwell Publishing who had a part in my journey, big or small, I needed all of you. My dream wouldn't have come to fruition without everyone. Shaheen Merah, you are the one who planted the seed and told me that I was holding in my hands, if I chose to publish it, a children's story book. I will forever be thankful that I had you as my teacher. Erin Ball, you made the journey of becoming a first-time author virtually pain free! It was a pleasure to have your talent and ambition on this journey. Stefanie St. Denis, thank you for your incredible illustrations, artistic talents and most of all your patience. Special thanks to Samantha Paul for the book design and Scott Lunn for his assistance.